A Storybook by
Nancy E. Krulik

from a
screenplay by Mark Saltzman

based on a
screenplay by Simon Sheen

SCHOLASTIC INC.
New York Toronto London Auckland Sydney

TRISTAR PICTURES PRESENTS A SHEEN PRODUCTION IN ASSOCIATION WITH BEN-AMI/LEEDS PRODUCTIONS A CHARLES T. KANGANIS FILM "3 NINJAS KICK BACK" VICTOR WONG MAX ELLIOTT SLADE SEAN FOX EVAN BONIFANT AND SAB SHIMONO MUSIC BY RICHARD MARVIN EXECUTIVE PRODUCERS SIMON SHEEN YORAM BEN-AMI BASED ON A SCREENPLAY BY SIMON SHEEN PG PARENTAL GUIDANCE SUGGESTED SCREENPLAY BY MARK SALTZMAN PRODUCED BY JAMES KANG MARTHA CHANG ARTHUR LEEDS DIRECTED BY CHARLES T. KANGANIS

Cover photo by Ron Slenzak.
Interior photos supplied by
Youshiharu Nushida and Yoshiyaki Shina.



ISBN 0-590-48495-8

 Published by Scholastic Inc.
Book designed by Ursula Herzog

12 11 10 9 8 7 6 5 4 3 2 1 4 5 6 7 8 9/9

Printed in the U.S.A. 09

First Scholastic printing, May 1994

# Chapter 1

The evil ninja crept quietly between the trees. The heavy summer leaves were the perfect cover for his black uniform. Even his red-and-black ninja mask was hidden from view.

Rocky could sense that the evil ninja was near. Without hesitation, he climbed to a high branch on a nearby tree. He watched . . . and waited. Sooner or later, the evil ninja would show himself. And when he did — Rocky would be there to stop him!

Then, suddenly, the evil ninja darted out onto the path! Rocky swung down from the tree, his leg poised to kick at the evil ninja. The ninja dropped and rolled into the underbrush, avoiding Rocky's outstretched leg. Rocky made another lunge at the ninja, but he ducked out of the way. Rocky slid into the dirt. When the dust cleared, the ninja was gone.

The evil ninja was not finished with his mission. There were still two more young ninja warriors to fight. The evil ninja made his way to a nearby stream. There, he grabbed a stick and balanced himself on a log. The evil ninja waited patiently. He was certain that Colt, his next victim, would be coming soon.

The evil ninja did not have long to wait. In an instant, Colt dropped down from an overhead branch. He swung his *bo* stick like a baseball bat, hoping to hit the evil ninja. But the evil ninja reacted quickly. He darted back and forth, managing to both avoid the *bo* stick and force Colt from the log.

As he ran off, the evil ninja smiled. Two down, one to go, he thought. The evil ninja moved cautiously through the woods once more. Tum Tum, the third and final ninja warrior, hid in a bush. As he waited, Tum Tum munched on a piece of red licorice. When the evil ninja approached, Tum Tum leaped out at him. But the evil ninja did a perfect backflip, completely avoiding Tum Tum's attack.

Rocky and Colt ran to Tum Tum's aid. The three warriors all grabbed sticks and prepared to fight the evil ninja — three against one! With a wild yell, they attacked. But the ninja had a secret weapon. He unleashed a smoke bomb. The air became dark and thick with smoke. The stench from the smoke was awful. Yet the three ninja warriors fought on, swinging their sticks with all their might. It wasn't until the smoke cleared that the warriors realized they had been fighting themselves! The evil ninja had disappeared in the cloud of smoke!

Tum Tum was the first to remove his ninja mask. "Why did you get in my way, Colt?" he asked his brother. "I had him!"

Colt removed his mask. "You

didn't get near him, Tum Tum."

"Did too, didn't I, Rocky?"

Rocky removed his mask and looked to the tree branches up above. "Looks like Grandpa wins again," he said to his two younger brothers.

Up above, the evil ninja, who wasn't really evil at all, smiled down at them. The whole fight was a lesson — to teach the boys how to be the best ninja warriors they possibly could. Their teacher was their grandfather, Mori. Mori had been the boys' ninja instructor for many years now.

But the boys' grandfather was getting older. And he had taught them everything he could. It was time for them to move on and learn from more experienced teachers. It was time for them to travel to Japan.

"I must go there next week, to my hometown of Konang," Mori explained to the boys later, as they sat in his cabin. "I have arranged for you to come with me, to study with the grand master."

Mori went over to a wall in the kitchen. Then he pried a panel in the wall loose. The boys stared with fascination. There was a secret compartment hidden in the wall!

"Wow! I never knew that was there!" Rocky said in surprise.

"That was the point." His grandfather laughed. Carefully, Mori reached into the compartment and pulled out an ancient dagger. The boys looked at the dagger with respect. They knew that this had to be an important ninja tool.

"Fifty years ago ... I was about your age," Mori began. "I fought for the honor of receiving this dagger. There was a legend about the dagger and a samurai sword — that they could open the door to a cave

of gold, laden with riches. Many believed the story. Koga, the boy I defeated, was one of them. When he lost, he tried to steal the dagger from me."

"What happened to that kid?" Colt asked.

Mori shrugged his shoulders. His mind raced back fifty years. It was a difficult match. At one point, Mori's sword had even sliced Koga's cheek. Mori wondered if Koga still bore the scar of the battle. "Who knows?" he answered. "Just boys playing a long time ago. But now, I am the old master. I must take the dagger back, and present it to the winner of the ninja tournament just as it was presented to me fifty years ago."

Tum Tum was so excited, he stopped eating his candy! "What about the cave of gold, Grandpa?" he asked. "Can we visit it when we go to Japan?"

Colt stared at him. Sometimes his little brother could be so stupid! "Weren't you listening, twerp? We need the sword to get in, too."

"Bigger twerp," Tum Tum answered.

"Boys, boys..." Mori interrupted. "It is just a legend. There is no cave of gold, and the sword — no one knows where it is."

## Chapter 2

That wasn't true. Someone did indeed know where the samurai sword was. And at that very moment, in far-off Japan, a ninja named Koga was entering a museum, ready to steal it!

Koga moved as quietly and gracefully as a leopard in the dark, empty museum. His eyes searched through the cases of swords until he found the one for which he had come. Then he pulled a *shiruken* star from his pouch. With a twist of his wrist, Koga used the sharp star to cut open the glass case. His eyes glistened as he grabbed the sword and ran from the building. Finally, the sword of Konang was his! He had been waiting for this moment for fifty years — since Mori Shintaro had defeated him in ninja battle!

Koga had never forgotten the legend of the cave. He knew he needed the dagger to enter. He also knew that Mori had the dagger. And Koga would stop at nothing to get it from him!

## Chapter 3

Baseball was the one thing the Douglas boys liked almost as much as ninja — all except Tum Tum, of course, who liked food better than just about anything! And they could be pretty good at baseball when their tempers didn't get in the way of their playing. Unfortunately, their tempers almost *always* got in the way of their playing. Colt's temper was the worst of all. And everyone in the baseball league knew it.

That's why, during the last game in the league championship playoffs, the other team tried purposely to make Colt angry. When Colt went up to bat, the catcher untied Colt's shoes. Then he put dirt in Colt's batting helmet. Colt felt his temper flare, but he kept his cool. Finally, the pitcher threw a wild pitch. The ball slammed into Colt's batting helmet. That was it! Colt had had enough! He cracked the bat over his knee and lunged at the pitcher, using the two pieces of the bat as ninja sticks.

The battle was on! Boys from both teams raced onto the field and began fighting. The umpire finally had to stop the game.

"This is the most disgraceful display I've ever seen in any baseball game," the umpire said. "I am suspending this game for a week to give you a chance to calm down. We'll start the game over next Sunday."

*Sunday?* Tum Tum jumped. "How can we replay the game next Sunday?" he said to his brothers. "We'll be in Japan with Grandpa."

# Chapter 4

The next day, the three ninjas gathered at their grandfather's cabin. While the boys were cooking dinner, Mori was on the phone with the travel agent, arranging for the trip to Japan.

"That's right, to Japan," he said to the travel agent. "How many tickets? I'm not sure . . ."

"Get one for me," Tum Tum shouted out.

"No!" Colt shouted.

"It's Japan, Colt," Rocky said to his brother. "How often do we get a chance like this? You want to throw it away?"

Colt glared at Rocky. "What about winning a baseball championship; you want to throw that away?"

"I want to go," Tum Tum butted in.

"Your vote doesn't count," Colt argued.

"It does too," Tum Tum answered back.

There wasn't much he could do about Tum Tum. But Colt knew just how to convince his older brother to stay. "Rocky, you could pitch the winning game," he smiled. "What do you think Lisa DiMarino would think of that?"

Lisa DiMarino! She was the girl of Rocky's dreams. That settled it. The vote was two to one. The three ninjas were staying to play baseball.

Their decision made Mori very sad. But he knew that to truly study the art of ninja, the boys had to make their own decisions.

"Just one ticket, please," he said.

Tum Tum walked over to his grandfather. "Grandpa . . . I voted to go." He said proudly.

Mori smiled. "I'm glad, Tum Tum," he said. "That means you want to continue your ninja training."

"Well . . . I really wanna go there to learn to be a sumo wrestler. You know how much those guys get to eat every day?"

Mori sighed. He went to the front door and grabbed his car keys. "Don't burn dinner," he called to the boys as he left to run a few last-minute errands for his trip. "And clean up this mess."

"By the time you come back, it'll be spotless," Tum Tum answered.

*Splat!* A tomato fell from the ceiling and landed right on Mori's head. Spotless? Somehow he doubted it.

# Chapter 5

Mori drove off down the road from his cabin. Just behind him was an old, beat-up, mobile home. Inside were three young grungy rock musicians, named Glam, Slam, and Vinnie. They were busy talking about the name for their new band. But that's not what they were supposed to be doing. They were *supposed* to be robbing Mori's house. Glam, Slam, and Vinnie were being paid by Koga to steal Mori's dagger.

"Stop, I think that's him!" Glam shouted out as Mori's car drove past. Slam slammed on the brakes. Glam and Vinnie popped out of their seats and rammed into the windshield.

"It's the old guy," Glam said. "The one we're stealing *this* from." Glam held up a picture of the dagger.

"Whoa . . . no wonder your uncle's paying us twenty grand. That's a nice letter opener!" Slam laughed.

Glam checked to make sure Mori wasn't coming back. "He's gone," he said. "That means the cabin's empty."

# Chapter 6

That was a serious mistake. The cabin wasn't empty at all. The three ninjas were inside.

"You are really being a jerk to Grandpa," Rocky was saying.

"Me? You wanted to stay, too." Colt answered.

*Buzz! Buzz!* Suddenly, the alarm system sounded. Lights flashed across the cabin.

"Somebody's coming," Rocky whispered to his brothers.

"Robbers," Colt suggested.

"Or maybe somebody's lost," Tum Tum said.

"Ninjas should always be prepared for battle," Rocky said. "Or to give directions."

The boys looked cautiously out the window. They could hear everything the "visitors" were saying.

"As long as we're in there, let's bag any hardware — CD player, speakers, TV . . ." Vinnie said.

The boys looked at each other.

"Directions?" Colt asked.

"I don't think so," they all said together.

"You with us?" Rocky asked Colt.

Colt nodded and gave a thumbs-up sign.

"Let's murderlize 'em!" Tum Tum shouted.

Tum Tum opened the refrigerator door, searching for ammunition. "Let's see what we have for our guests," he murmured, grabbing eggs, whipped cream, and a banana cream pie. Tum Tum grinned. These guys would never know what hit them!

Rocky quietly climbed a tree and watched, as Slam and Vinnie grabbed a crowbar from the mobile home and prepared to break down the front door.

"Okay, on three," Vinnie said. "One, two . . ."

"Three!" Rocky said to himself as he yanked a fishing line as hard as he could. The line opened the door, sending Vinnie and Slam crashing into the cabin. Slam's head went right through a chair! And when he tried to pull off the chair, he stepped on Vinnie's hand!

Slam spotted a desk across the room. "Hey, look! A desk!" he said to Vinnie.

"So?"

"Well, if you had a letter opener, wouldn't you put it in there?" Slam rifled through the desk. But all he could find was a plain metal letter opener.

Outside, Glam was getting bored. He pulled out a toy microphone, tossed his bleached-white hair, and pretended to sing to a screaming crowd.

*Bam! Bam!* Two pinecones came pounding down on Glam's waiting head.

Inside, Vinnie and Slam weren't having much luck, either. Slam went into the kitchen and spotted the pantry. Now that's a good hiding place, he thought. He opened the door —

*Spritz!* Soda water came shooting out of the pantry door. Slam screamed out in surprise. The door slammed shut.

Cautiously, Slam opened the door again. A dozen eggs pelted rapid-fire right into his face. But before he could say anything, the pantry door shut once more.

Now Slam was really mad! He wiped the yellow goo from his eyes, yanked open the pantry door, and — *KABOOM!* Tum Tum, the human missile, launched out headfirst! He landed squarely into Slam's belly! Slam bounced backward, then forward, and landed in a huge, gooey cream pie!

"Mmm . . . lemon meringue," Slam said.

"Banana cream, bozo!" Tum Tum shouted. Boy, these guys couldn't even tell a lemon from a banana, Tum Tum thought. Some thieves!

"Vinnie!" Slam screamed upstairs. "The house ain't empty!"

"What are you talking about?" Vinnie answered from the bedroom. "There's nobody here!"

Just then, the quilt on the bed jumped. So did Vinnie. He'd had no idea that Colt was under the quilt. In a split second, Colt kicked out his leg. His foot landed squarely on Vinnie's forehead.

"Let's get out of here while we're still standing," Slam yelled to Vinnie. And with that, they took off out of the house.

"Come and see us again sometime," Tum Tum said as the mobile home sped away. "We'll leave a light on!"

## Chapter 7

When Mori arrived home, he was in shock. But not because of the bad guys — he didn't even know about them. Mori couldn't believe the mess inside his cabin. Chairs were broken, food was everywhere, and there was a huge pile of pine-cones lining the driveway.

"This is spotless?" he called out.

The three ninjas came sliding down the staircase. They were so excited, they all started to speak at once.

"There were these guys! They wanted to rob the cabin! We got rid of them!"

"We took care of them Grandpa. You should have seen it!" Rocky exclaimed.

"Yeah, they finally gave up and ran away," Tum Tum added.

Mori shook his head. "Next time, call the police," he said.

Colt looked confused. "But Grandpa," he said. "We used everything you taught us. We were great!"

"A true ninja does not brag about his skills," Mori said. "But I forgot, you don't want any more advice from me," he added sadly.

The boys looked down at the ground in shame. For the first time, they realized how much they had hurt their grandfather by choosing baseball over ninja. But it was too late to do anything about that now.

* * *

All too soon, it was time for Mori to leave for Japan. He packed his clothes in one suitcase, and placed the ceremonial dagger and his wallet in a ninja bag. The ninja bag was very special to Mori. He had given one just like it to each of his grandsons.

Tum Tum was especially partial to his ninja bag. After all, it could hold an awful lot of candy! And candy was something Tum Tum never went anywhere without! He filled his ninja bag with candy and Ding Dongs and put it in the car next to Mori's luggage.

Once the car was loaded, Mori, the three ninjas, and their parents drove off to the airport. They didn't even notice the mobile home following them down the highway.

At the airport, Mori picked up his luggage and hugged his family good-bye. When they had driven out of sight, Mori went into the terminal to wait for his plane.

Vinnie, Slam, and Glam watched him go inside.

"Hey! There he goes with the bag!" Glam jumped up excitedly.

Slam turned to Vinnie. "Where's he goin'?"

Vinnie shrugged. "I don't know, but we're goin' too!"

"Who's goin'?" Glam asked. He'd forgotten what they were talking about. But Vinnie had just caught on. "The guy with the bag," he said.

"All right!" they cheered. "Vacation time!"

## Chapter 8

Tokyo had changed quite a bit in the years since Mori had last been to Japan. Still, as he looked out the window of his taxicab, Mori thought the city looked beautiful. He sat back and relaxed, as the driver wove through the traffic on the city street.

Then, out of nowhere, a rented car swerved from the left lane! It bashed into the taxi so hard that the trunk of the cab popped open. Mori was thrown backwards from the impact of the hit.

Glam jumped out of the rented car. "Open season on luggage!" he cried out as he grabbed Mori's ninja bag. Mori looked out and saw the grunger run off.

But try as he might, Mori could not get out of the taxi. Finally, he slumped down in his seat, unconscious.

Glam, Slam, and Vinnie didn't wait around to find out what happened to the old man. They hurried straight to Koga's office. They were eager to give him the dagger — and collect their $20,000 reward!

"Greetings, Uncle," Glam said to Koga. "We did your bidding and we've got the goods right here!"

"Quiet, fool! Give it to me!" Koga said, reaching for the bag. He quickly turned it over, but there was no dagger inside. There were, however, licorice, jelly beans, Ding Dongs, and candy bars! Mori had taken Tum Tum's bag to Japan by mistake!

"You have failed me again!" Koga shouted. "But I am prepared to give you another chance. Find out where that dagger is and bring it to me!"

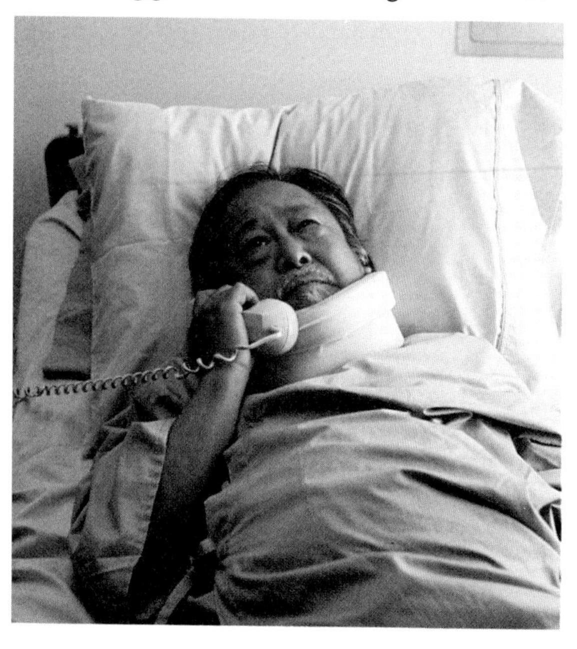

# Chapter 9

Back in the United States, the three ninjas were doing what they always did when they were home alone — arguing. They were so busy with their disagreement, they didn't even hear the telephone ring. It was a good thing the answering machine was on.

"Boys, I'm all right," the voice on the other end said. "But I'm in the hospital in Tokyo."

Rocky leaped up and picked up the phone receiver. He didn't even stop to turn off the answering machine!

"I was in a tiny car accident," Mori explained. "Just a few bruises. I'm okay, but my luggage got stolen. All of it. Even the dagger."

After assuring the boys once more that he was all right, Mori hung up the phone.

"Did he say who hit him?" Colt asked Rocky.

"Some guy with white hair," Rocky answered.

"Like that jerko metalhead at the cabin?" Tum Tum asked.

Colt and Rocky stared at each other. For once, Tum Tum had a point.

"Oh, no!" Rocky cried out.

"Those guys are in Japan!" Colt said.

Suddenly, Tum Tum let out a bloodcurdling cry.

"This isn't my bag!" Tum Tum said, holding up a ninja bag. "It's Grandpa's! And look!" Tum Tum reached in the bag and pulled out the dagger.

Mori was in big trouble!

"We gotta go there, right away!" Colt said.

Rocky looked at his brother with surprise. "But Colt, what about the baseball game?"

"That's just a game," Colt said. "This is Grandpa. Blood is thicker than Gatorade."

That settled it. The three ninjas had to go to Japan. But first they had to buy airplane tickets. Rocky searched through Mori's bag until he found a credit card. Rocky knew that using someone's credit card was wrong, but this was an emergency. Quickly, Rocky called the ticket clerk at the airport and ordered three children's fares to Tokyo.

"What is the name on the card?" the ticket clerk asked.

"Mori Shintaro. He's my grandfather," Rocky told her.

"I'm afraid we'll need his authorization," the ticket clerk explained. "Is he there?"

Oh, no! Rocky hadn't counted on that. Then he spotted his grandfather's answering machine.

"Is Grandpa's message still on the tape?" he whispered to Colt.

Colt nodded. He knew just what Rocky was thinking. He pressed rewind on the machine.

"Hello." Mori's voice came on over the speaker.

"Mr. Shintaro, how are you today?" the ticket clerk asked.

Colt fast-forwarded to another part of the tape.

"I'm fine."

"That's nice," the ticket clerk said. "I just took a reservation on your card by a nice young man —"

"My grandson," interrupted the answering machine.

Rocky breathed a sigh of relief. It was working! The boys had their airplane tickets.

There was, however, the little matter of what to tell their parents. There was always the possibility that they wouldn't want the boys to go to Japan all by themselves.

Rocky couldn't take that chance. The boys had to be out of the house by the time their parents returned!

"Okay, we gotta get in gear," he said to his brothers. "I'll write a note to Mom and Dad. You find all the money in the house," he told Colt. "You call a cab," he told Tum Tum.

Rocky had a feeling that his parents would be more than a little upset when they found out the boys had taken off for Tokyo without permission. But by the time they found the note, the boys would be flying over the Pacific Ocean on their way to Japan.

## Chapter 10

The flight to Tokyo was a long one. Rocky and Colt spent the hours trying to nap. Tum Tum spent the hours looking for the woman with the peanuts.

When they finally arrived at the Tokyo airport, the boys were amazed. They had never seen so many people in one place. They were about to find a taxi when they heard a loud scream. A robber was trying to steal an old woman's purse. Lucky for her, the three ninjas were standing by. Colt reached in his bag and pulled out a baseball. He tossed it to Rocky. Rocky wound up for the pitch, let the ball fly, and . . . *BONK!* A perfect hit! The ball bashed the robber in the head. He fell to the ground and let go of the purse. The old woman was so grateful, she gave the boys a ride to the hospital in her limousine!

"Aaaargh!"

As the boys walked down the hospital hallway to Mori's room, they heard a painful cry.

"Grandpa's in trouble!" Rocky shouted. The ninjas rushed down the hall and into their grandfather's room. They were ready for battle!

But there was no battle to be had. Mori's enemy was just the nurse — she had given Mori a shot of medication.

Mori looked up as the boys entered the room. He was surprised to see them. "Boys! Boys!" he called out happily. "What are you doing here?"

"There's something really important to tell you," Rocky began.

"We think you are in a lot of

danger," Colt continued.

"The guy you said stole your luggage? The guy with the white hair?" Rocky added.

"He's the same guy who tried to rob the cabin!" Colt explained. "We think those guys were after the dagger, Grandpa."

Mori looked sadly at the floor. "Well, they have it now," he sighed.

Colt and Rocky looked at each other and grinned. They knew that the thieves had nothing but licorice, jelly beans, candy bars, and Ding Dongs.

Rocky took the dagger out of the bag.

"You took Tum Tum's bag by mistake," Rocky laughed.

"And they got my Ding Dongs," Tum Tum said angrily.

Mori beamed. The dagger was safe after all. Then something occured to him — how did the boys come all this way alone? As soon as the boys told him how they had dashed to the airport and left a note for their parents, Mori made the boys call home.

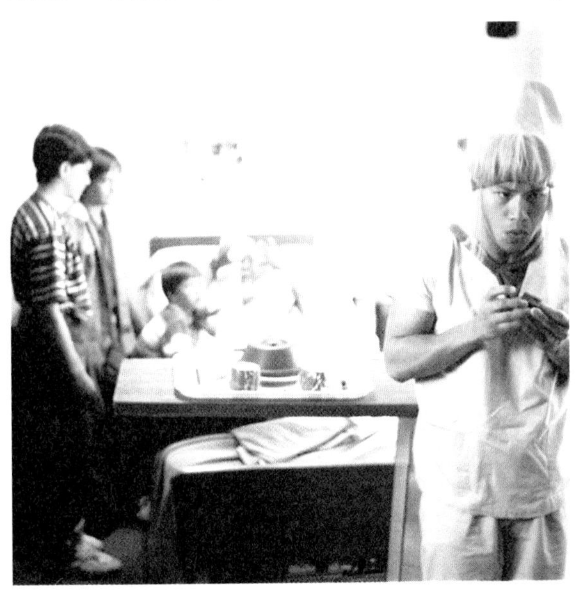

Just as Rocky had suspected, his parents were really angry with the three ninjas. But they agreed that the boys should stay in Japan with Mori. They would discuss the whole thing as soon as their sons arrived home. In the meantime, the ninjas were to call home every day at two o'clock.

Rocky breathed a sigh of relief, as Mori hung up the phone. At least *that* was over.

"The tournament is going on in Konang now," Mori told his grandsons. "You boys take the dagger there for me and present it to the winner of the competition.

"They're releasing me from the hospital in two days. I'll meet you there then."

The three ninjas nodded. They had a mission, and nothing would stand in their way.

Still, it wouldn't be as easy a mission as the boys and Mori believed. They didn't know it, but Glam, Slam, and Vinnie had taped their entire conversation. And what Glam, Slam, and Vinnie knew, Koga was certain to find out.

# Chapter 11

The Konang tournament was in full swing by the time the three ninjas arrived at the *dojo*. Brightly colored banners hung from the ceilings. Team members in brightly colored uniforms paraded before the cheering crowd. Parents with video cameras proudly photographed their young ninja stars.

The three ninjas took a place in the bleachers and watched a few of the matches. Clearly the best contestant was Number 7. All of Number 7's moves were clean and neat. And Number 7's ninja scream was the loudest, deepest cry the boys had ever heard.

"He's really good," Rocky said, impressed. He was so fascinated, he didn't even notice Colt getting up off the bench.

One by one, Number 7 defeated each and every opponent. The only one left for him to compete against was Number 16.

"Hey . . . that guy's not bad!" Tum Tum said as he watched this final battle.

"He's kind of wild, though. Like Colt," Rocky noted.

The boys looked at one another. "COLT!"

Tum Tum started to run toward the mat. "Come on!" he called to Rocky. "He's gonna get his brains splattered."

"Stay here," Rocky said calmly.

"Maybe this is the lesson Grandpa had in mind."

Colt did his best, but he was no match for Number 7. After a series of brilliant ninja moves, Colt went down on the mat. Number 7 was the champion of the tournament!

Colt and Number 7 removed their ninja masks. Boy, was Colt in for a surprise! Number 7 was . . .

"A girl!" Colt shouted out in shock.

"A girl!" Tum Tum said with disgust.

"A girl," Rocky repeated. And a cute girl at that.

"If she's the winner . . . does that mean we give her this?" Tum Tum asked, pointing to the bag that held the dagger.

Just then, the grand master came over to congratulate Miyo, the winner of the tournament. The grand master was quite an impressive sight to see. He wore a ceremonial robe and mask — similar to those worn hundreds of years ago. And, like the grand masters of times gone by, he wore no shoes.

"Whoa . . . look at those feet. I think he's Fred Flintstone." Tum Tum laughed.

"Even in Japan, you're a dufus," Colt answered.

"Maybe. But at least I didn't get beat by a girl!"

"I'm still better than you!"

"Shut up, spaz."

Miyo put out her hand to shake Colt's. "You are a worthy opponent, Spaz," she said.

Tum Tum giggled. Colt glared at him. "No. It's Colt. This is Rocky and Tum Tum."

When Miyo found out that they had no place to stay in Konang, she and her mother offered to take the boys home with them. But first, they had to go to a very important place.

## Chapter 12

*SMACK!* The baseball popped up in the air and then went foul. Miyo wiped her brow in frustration. The important place Miyo's mother had taken them to was a baseball field. Miyo was trying out for her local team.

"Every year she is the only girl to try out," Miyo's mother explained to the boys.

Rocky watched as Miyo ran onto the field. The new batter hit a pop fly in her direction. Miyo raced toward the ball. The baseball landed in her glove . . . but dropped right out again.

She's not too bad, Rocky thought to himself. With a little practice, she could make the team.

Miyo walked over to the foul line. "He says to come back when I learn to catch," Miyo explained.

"Maybe next year, little butterfly," her mother said gently.

"Hey . . . I got an idea. You teach us ninja . . . we teach you baseball," Rocky suggested.

Miyo smiled at him. What a great idea!

All the following day, Miyo and the boys worked together. She taught them to develop grace and style in their ninja exercises. They taught her to catch a ball with such accuracy that even a raw egg would not break in her hands.

Miyo invited the three ninjas into her favorite practice *dojo*. There she presented them with a true sign of honor: new blue, green, and yellow robes. Rocky presented Miyo with a true sign of honor, too: his Dragons baseball shirt.

# Chapter 13

The boys were finally beginning to relax and enjoy Japan. They could not know that their relaxation was soon to come to an end. Koga had already arrived in Konang. And as Rocky prepared to learn enough Japanese to meet the grand master, Koga was making some preparations of his own.

That night, Koga snuck into the grand master's kitchen. He poured a small packet of sleeping powder into the master's tea. Then he hid behind a screen and watched the grand master take the tea from the kitchen and sit quietly for a private tea ceremony. Koga grinned as the grand master took his first sip from the delicate china teacup.

Almost immediately, the grand master started to cough. Then he fell down, unconscious.

# Chapter 14

The next morning, the boys were too excited to eat. All they wanted to do was get to the *dojo* and have a lesson from the grand master.

The boys and Miyo arrived at the *dojo* early. They wanted to be there when the grand master arrived. They didn't have to wait long before a man in ceremonial robes and a grand master mask entered the room.

"So you are the grandsons of Mori Shintaro," he said.

Tum Tum was sure there was something different about this man. "Hey . . . how come you didn't speak English at the tournament?" he asked suspiciously.

The man behind the mask didn't miss a beat. "In front of other people? They would not understand us. It would be rude. It is clear you have much to learn about Japanese customs," he said.

"We are here to learn, sir," Rocky replied.

The older man nodded. "But first . . . do you have the dagger that your grandfather gave you?"

Rocky thought the grand master would have wanted them to wait for Mori to arrive before they gave him the dagger. But Tum Tum reached into his bag and pulled out the dagger. As he walked up to hand it over, Tum Tum noticed something odd.

"Weren't you shorter the other day?" he said suddenly.

"He's a fake!" Miyo cried out.

"SCRAMBLE!" Tum Tum yelled.

Koga called to his *yakuzas*. "After them!" he ordered.

The *yakuzas* chased after the kids. There was only one place they could have gone — into the *dojo's* second, smaller gym.

The *yakuzas* weren't playing at ninja games. They meant business! On their belts they wore long, sharp ninja swords. One of them also wore a portable phone — just in case of an emergency.

The evil *yakuzas* burst into the gym with an angry yell, ready for battle! But what they found there stopped them dead in their tracks. The room was completely empty! Where could the young ninjas have gone?

"Eeeeya!" Miyo, Colt, and Rocky swung down from the beams in the ceiling. *Boom! Boom! Boom!* Together they kicked each of the three *yakuzas* in the head.

Two of the *yakuzas* wobbled slowly and fell to the ground. But the third, and strongest, stood tall. He reached to his side to draw his sword. Whoops! He grabbed his portable telephone instead.

"What are you going to do, *talk* us to death?" Colt said, while he laughed in the *yakuza's* face.

The *yakuza* was embarrassed. But he was a trained ninja. He gathered his senses quickly and drew his sword. Miyo, Colt, and Rocky grabbed *bo* sticks from the wall of the gym. Swiftly, they went into action battling the *yakuzas*.

But where was Tum Tum? He was still hiding on the ceiling beams. And he, too, was ready to use his weapon of choice. In Tum Tum's case the weapon wasn't a *bo* stick, a sword, or a *shiruken* star. Tum Tum's favorite weapon was . . . food! He leaped from beam to beam pelting the *yakuzas* with jelly beans.

Tum Tum was in the middle of throwing down a handful of red, black, and purple jelly beans when he heard a beeping sound. It was his watch alarm. It was two o'clock. He had to call his mom and dad and let them know he was okay.

Tum Tum grabbed onto a rope that was hanging from the ceiling. He swung down, grabbed the cellular phone off the *yakuza's* belt, and swung back up to the rafters.

Quickly, Tum Tum dialed his home phone number.

"Hi, Mom! It's me!" Tum Tum said when his mother answered.

"It's about time! You're five minutes late!" his mother answered.

Tum Tum looked down at the battle on the gym floor. "I was hung up!" he explained.

It took a lot of fancy swinging on Tum Tum's part to make sure that each of his brothers got a chance to talk to their folks, but eventually he did it. Rocky was the last to speak. No sooner had he hung up the phone, when it rang again.

"It's for you!" Rocky cried out, shoving the phone into a *yakuza's* mouth! Instinctively, the other two *yakuzas* reached over to answer the still-ringing phone.

The four young ninjas took the opportunity to run from the *yakuzas*. Miyo led the way. "There's a secret passageway to the outside," she said.

Miyo and the boys ran down the passageway. When they reached the end, Miyo kicked open the door. There, waiting for them, was Koga.

"As I learned here," Koga said pointing to the *dojo*, "never enter a battle you can't win."

The four ninjas were trapped. They had no choice but to go with Koga to his hideout. Koga and his guards forced the young ninjas down into a dark, musty jail cell and slammed the door.

"I just wish I was home," Tum Tum moaned. "I want to see Mom and Dad. I want to be in my own house, and have a real cheeseburger with real cheese."

"I knew this would get around to food," Colt snapped.

Rocky knew he would have to take charge if they were ever to escape.

"What is a ninja?" Rocky asked his brothers and Miyo. "A body . . ." he began.

"A spirit," Colt added.

"A mind," Miyo continued.

"A heart," Tum Tum finished, even though his was breaking.

They smiled at one another. Somehow, they would get out of this awful place.

* * *

Upstairs, Koga was giving Slam, Glam, and Vinnie their next mission — kidnap Mori Shintaro.

"I have the dagger and the samurai sword," he explained. "But they tell me nothing. Only one man knows their secret — that is Mori Shintaro. Are you capable of kidnapping an old man? A *hospitalized* old man?" Koga asked sarcastically.

The truth was, Glam, Slam, and Vinnie were not capable even of that! They went to the hospital, prepared to kidnap Mori. But even though he was in a wheelchair, the three dumb grungers were no match for the old ninja. All Slam, Vinnie, and Glam wound up bringing home from the hospital were a few fractured bones!

Koga was prepared for his nephew and his friends to fail once again. That's why he sent his largest and most trusted sumo wrestler, Ishikawa, to finish the job.

## Chapter 15

Ishikawa threw Mori into a dark room.

"Why have you brought me here? Why?" Mori asked.

Suddenly the door opened, allowing a sliver of light to pass through into the room. A tall man stood at the entranceway.

"Who are you?" Mori asked.

"Just a boy you knew in Konang," Koga said, turning his scarred cheek toward Mori.

"Koga?" Mori asked with surprise. "So this is what has become of you. I remember well your greed."

Koga laughed. *He* was in control now. "But you must remember more, old friend. I have the sword. I have your dagger. But the cave of gold . . . where is it?"

Mori looked at Koga with pity. How sad that this man had never gotten over his obsession with wealth and power.

"I remember nothing about the cave," Mori said slowly. He did not want to reveal the ancient secret of

the cave to such an evil man.

Koga got angry. He was a man who was used to getting what he wanted. He grabbed Mori and pushed him down the hall to the jail cell where the three ninjas and Miyo were held prisoner. The boys were overjoyed to see him.

"Get us out, Grandpa! Please!" Tum Tum cried.

Mori tried to smile reassuringly. "Don't worry. I will get you out," he said.

"The cave, where is the cave?" Koga insisted. "Do you wish to watch your grandchildren die?" he threatened.

"According to legend, the cave is beneath the Castle Hikone," Mori answered. "The sword and dagger are the keys. Now let my grandchildren free."

But Koga had no intention of freeing the children. "You have somewhere else to go first," he replied. "Castle Hikone."

The boys watched as the two men walked away. Their grandfather was a prisoner just like they were. It looked like the four ninjas were going to have to find their own way out of this mess. They looked around the cell. There were no windows and nothing they could use as weapons.

"Forget it, there's no way to escape," Tum Tum said.

Rocky grinned. He had a plan. "We don't have to," he said. "We just have to make it *look* like we did!"

The ninjas pulled off all of their bedsheets and knotted them together. They wanted it to look as though they had escaped from the cell. They talked about climbing out the window from between the bars. The guard outside the door chuckled as he listened to the kids plan their "escape." But then there was silence. The guard jumped to attention. Could the kids really have escaped?

The guard looked through the bars of the cell. The children *had* disappeared. Quickly, he unlocked the door and walked into the cell. *Kaboom!* Rocky swung down from the rafters and knocked out the guard. The others jumped down after him and ran from the cell.

It took only a few seconds for Koga's *yakuzas* to discover the escape. They followed the three ninjas and Miyo down the hall and out into the *dojo*. There was no safe place for the kids to go but up.

"The roof!" Miyo called out to them.

The *yakuzas* were right behind them. Quickly, Miyo slammed the door that led to the roof. But that door wouldn't keep the *yakuzas* out for long.

Miyo pointed out into the distance. "There, that's the Castle Hikone," Miyo said.

"How are we gonna get there?" Tum Tum asked.

Miyo looked around. Then she grinned. In the corner she saw two old wooden gliders.

"On the wings of eagles," she said.

Miyo helped strap the boys to

the gliders. Tum Tum and Colt shared one, she and Rocky shared the other. The four kids ran to the edge of the roof at top speed.

"JUMMMMMMP!" ordered Miyo.

## Chapter 16

Meanwhile, Koga and Mori were wandering down a dim passageway beneath the Castle Hikone. When they reached the end, they came up against a wall of solid rock.

Koga banged his hand against the wall in frustration. That's when he noticed the drawing on the wall. In the drawing, two ninja warriors were doing battle. One held a samurai sword, the other held a dagger. When he looked closer, Koga noticed a small slit in the drawing of the sword, and another in the drawing of the dagger. Carefully, he slipped the sword into one slit and the dagger into the other. The wall began to tremble. Then it opened ever so slowly, revealing yet another passageway. The passageway led first to an ancient dining room and then to another staircase.

Koga could barely conceal his excitement. The cave of gold was about to be to his!

* * *

By now, the three ninjas and Miyo had entered the castle. They headed down the same path that Mori and Koga had taken.

"Look, the dagger and the sword!" Rocky cried out. Rocky removed the weapons from the wall. "We may need them," he explained to the others.

"There's a staircase," Rocky pointed out. "There must be another level."

Tum Tum groaned. "I'm beginning to feel like a Mario Brother."

"You're beginning to look like one!" Colt laughed, looking at Tum Tum's round belly.

The stairway led the ninjas deep into a mine. It was so dark, they could barely see. Perhaps that is why they never noticed Ishikawa lurking in the shadows! The huge man came and blocked their path.

"Ki-Ya!" Rocky, Miyo, Colt, and Tum Tum screamed out in preparation for battle. The kids pounced on Ishikawa with all of their might. Their fists and feet flew in the air. But physically they were no match for the huge sumo. He fended off each and every one of the attacks. This wasn't going to be easy. It would take some *ninja-nuity*! Quickly, Rocky and Colt hoisted Tum Tum onto Ishikawa's broad shoulders. The huge man whirled around in circles, trying to grab the boy. It took a few spins, but eventually Ishikawa tossed Tum Tum back into his brothers' arms.

This *really* wasn't going to be easy!

The ninjas huddled for a quick strategy conference. When the huddle broke, Miyo began teasing Ishikawa.

"You're a stupid hippo!" she said. "Your mother's belly button sticks out!"

That made Ishikawa mad! He didn't like people saying things about his mother! Ishikawa raced after the girl like a bull in a ring. Miyo moved swiftly to the side and — *WHOMP!* — Ishikawa

ran headfirst into a solid wall and collapsed to the floor.

*   *   *

The kids raced down the passageway toward Mori and Koga. Four *yakuzas* trailed close behind. Rocky, Miyo, Colt, and Tum Tum followed the tunnel as far as it would take them. Every now and then, Colt would turn and give a good kick to one of the *yakuzas*.

Colt backed up a step without looking. He fell into a large burlap curtain. Suddenly, he found himself sliding downward! He shouted out in surprise.

Miyo, Rocky, and Tum Tum heard his cry. "We're coming!" they called after him.

Before they knew what was happening, the four young ninjas were sliding down a giant, stone chute that would lead them to the mythical cave of gold!

## Chapter 17

Koga and Mori were already in the glistening cave. Everywhere they looked, there were shimmering gemstones and bright, shining gold sculptures. This was all Koga had longed for since childhood. He wasn't about to share it with Mori.

The two old ninjas began to fight. In their minds, both men were back in that small *dojo* in Konang. This was a battle that neither man was prepared to lose.

Mori landed a kick straight to Koga's face. Koga's gun dropped to the floor. Instinctively, Koga lunged for the gun. Mori took the opportunity to dive on top of Koga. Both men grabbed the gun at the same time. Finally, Koga gained control and pointed the gun at Mori.

"AAAAAAH!" At just that moment Rocky, Colt, Tum Tum, and Miyo came flying down the chute, feet first, screaming all the way. They slammed into Koga and knocked the gun out of his hand. In the confusion, the gun accidentally went off. The room quaked from the force of the explosion. The gold roof threatened to fall in around them.

"Let's go!" Mori ordered.

"You mean scramble!" Tum Tum agreed.

Koga looked around him. A lifetime of dreams, he thought. I cannot let this go.

"If you were a real ninja, the gold wouldn't matter to you," Tum Tum shouted to him.

"You have taught your grandsons well, Mori." Koga said. "Quite honorable."

Mori looked at him with pity. "You were once honorable, too. Come with us, old friend."

Koga looked at Mori through new eyes. Mori was trying to save his life — in spite of everything that had just happened. Quickly, Koga followed the others up the staircase.

When they reached the top, they discovered that the stone entranceway had closed behind them. Only the sword and dagger would open it again. Rocky grabbed the sword and slipped it into the slot in the door. Tum Tum pulled the dagger from his bag, and did the same. The stone door shuddered open.

Rocky pulled the dagger from the door. Koga took the sword. But Koga could not keep the sword now. It had caused far too much evil. Without looking back, Koga threw the sword behind him. The door slammed shut. The cave of gold was locked away forever.

Tum Tum was the last to climb the steps to safety. As the others ran out ahead of him, the boy's foot got caught on an old wooden stair. The walls began to crumble around him. Tum Tum began to panic. Koga turned and stared at Tum Tum. Then he looked at the open doorway. Any second it could crumble, and he would die. Risking his own life, Koga reached out his hand and pulled Tum Tum free.

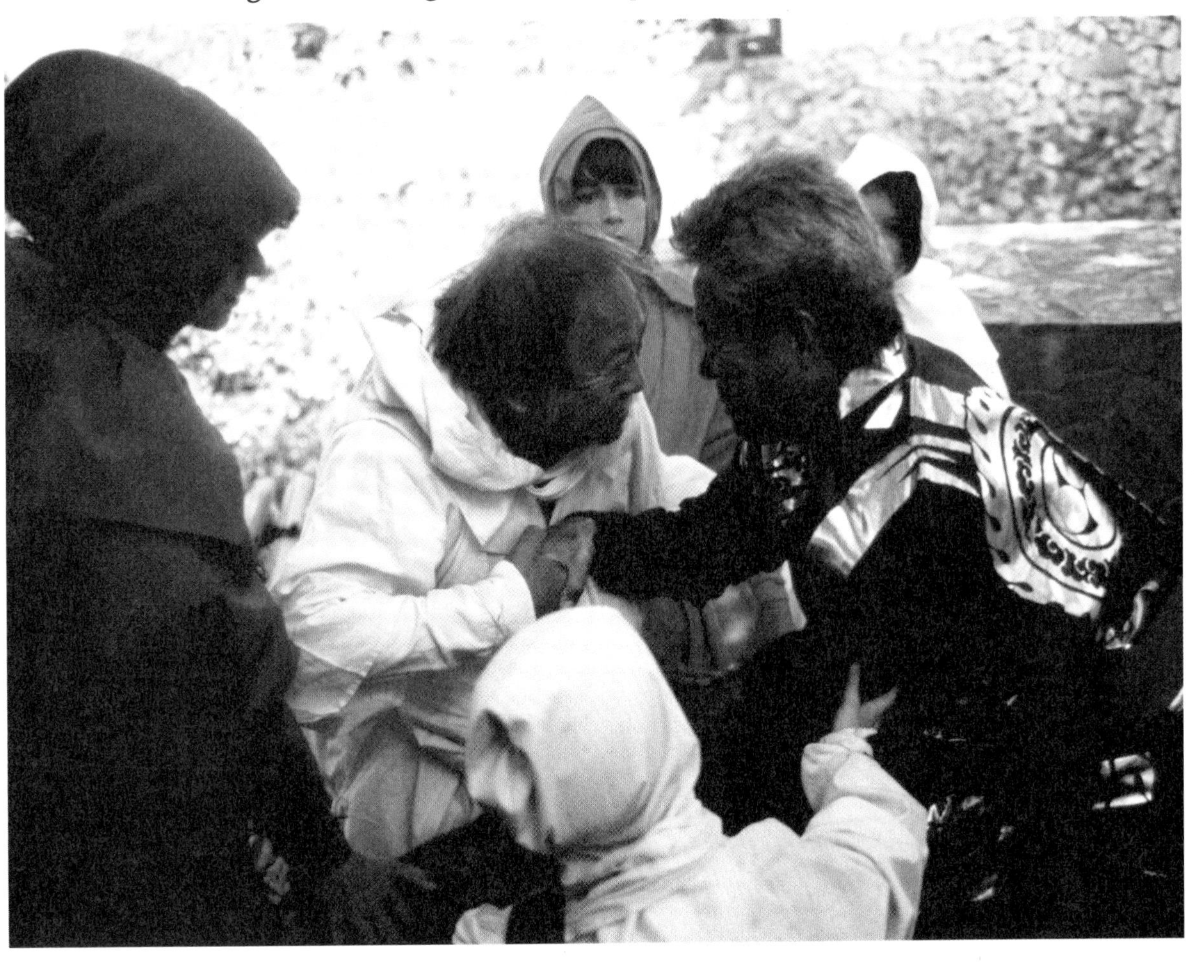

# Chapter 18

Outside, Koga turned to Mori, his old enemy who was now his friend. "A true ninja is free of all desire," he said. "It took me a long time to understand this, Mori Shintaro. From our days in Konang until this moment."

Mori turned to the boys. "Slow learner," he whispered. Then he grew serious. "You were brave ninjas, all of you."

Rocky turned toward Miyo. "Grandpa, this is Miyo. The champion of the Konang *Dojo*."

Mori handed Miyo the dagger. "Keep this dagger until the day that you, too, will present it to a young master," he said.

Miyo bowed and accepted the dagger.

Now that their mission had been completed, Colt's thoughts turned toward home. "Too bad we missed our game," he remarked. "But it was worth it."

Mori smiled. "I thought the game wasn't till Sunday."

Colt shrugged. "Today's Friday. . . . It's already tomorrow at home."

"But if we get a flight tonight —" Rocky added.

"One day back — we could make it!" Mori finished his thought.

"Scramble!" Tum Tum called out.

## Chapter 19

The three ninjas were very lucky that day. The plane was right on time, and there was very little traffic coming back from the airport. Still, they couldn't be sure that they would make it to the game on time.

"You can't play with only six players," the umpire was saying to the Dragons coach as the boys arrived.

"I guess I have no choice. We forfeit," the coach said.

"Play ball!"

The cry came from the bleachers. The three ninjas leaped onto the field.

The Mustangs were more than a little disappointed that the ninjas had returned in time. They certainly wouldn't have minded winning by forfeit. But they figured all they had to do was get the boys angry, and the game would be theirs anyhow.

The Mustangs certainly did their best. But nothing they could do would make the boys angry. Then, in the ninth inning, the Dragons center fielder was injured. If the Dragons didn't come up with another player, they would have to forfeit anyway.

That's when Number 21 jogged out onto the baseball field.

"Replacing Number 25 is Number 21," the announcer said. "Hmmm . . . this player doesn't seem to be on the roster."

Rocky concentrated on the strike zone. He pitched the ball. The batter hit a long drive to center field. Number 21 made a daredevil reach and caught the ball! Excited, Number 21 leaped into the air. The player's baseball cap flew off, and Miyo's long, brown hair fell to her shoulders! Miyo had won the game for the Dragons!

The game may have been over, but the Mustangs weren't finished yet.

"This game's gonna go extra innings in the parking lot," one of the players said, pushing Colt.

But Colt remained calm. "Tell you what," he said slowly. "One on one. Your best guy, and you can pick any one of us you want to fight against."

Darren, the biggest and meanest of the bullies, walked up to Miyo. "I pick *you*," he said. "You ruined my home run, girl."

Tum Tum laughed to himself. What a jerk, he thought. This guy just picked a fight with the winner of the Konang Ninja Tournament.

But Tum Tum didn't say that. Instead he said, "But she's just visiting. Pick me! I'll fight you."

Darren stood firm.

"Well, I tried," said Tum Tum.

"Kiiyaaaaa!" Miyo let out one of her famous ninja battle cries. Darren never had a chance!

The three ninjas stood back and laughed. Once again, *ninja-nuity* had come to the rescue!